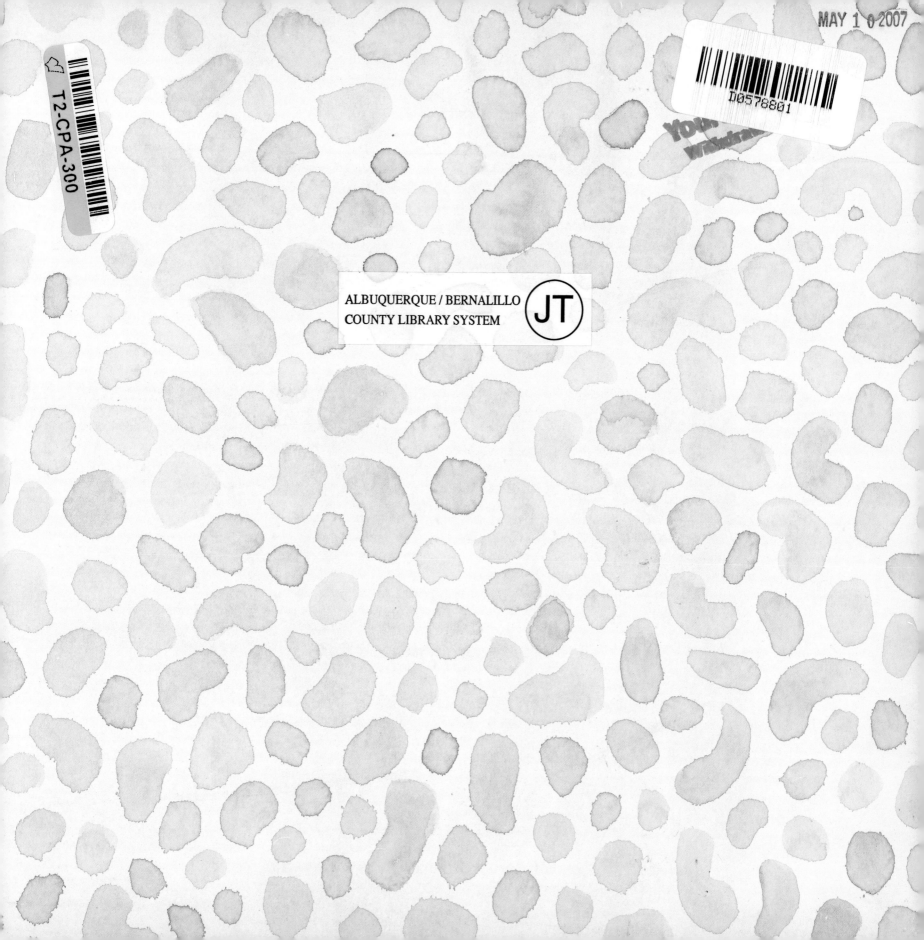

With love for Jessica, Makayla, Michelle, Nicole,
Elizabeth, and Carole
S. P.

For my sister Deborrah and my dear Srini
with love and thankfulness
C. J.

◉

Text copyright © 2007 by Shirley Parenteau
Illustrations copyright © 2007 by Cynthia Jabar

First edition 2007

Library of Congress Cataloging-in-Publication Data is available.

Library of Congress Catalog Card Number 2006049083

ISBN 978-0-7636-2394-4

2 4 6 8 10 9 7 5 3 1

Printed in China

This book was typeset in Alghera.
The illustrations were done in watercolor, aquapasto, and gouache.

Candlewick Press
2067 Massachusetts Avenue
Cambridge, Massachusetts 02140

visit us at www.candlewick.com

One Frog Sang

SHIRLEY PARENTEAU

illustrated by **CYNTHIA JABAR**

CANDLEWICK PRESS
CAMBRIDGE, MASSACHUSETTS

All the frogs hunkered low
while spring rains stormed by.
Then when the night became still . . .

1

One big frog leaped onto a high garden wall,
sucked in air, and blew out a song: Ka-blu-urp.

2

Two tiny frogs joined in
from a windowpane, shrieking,
Preep, preep,
in voices as loud as a crowd.

3

Three young frogs sang, Ribbit, ribbit,
from a puddle in the middle of a path.

4

Four spotted frogs sang,
Chirrup, chirrup,
from a tree trunk,
hugging the bark.

5

Five frogs sang, Rah-BEET,
from a birdbath where
a mirror moon swam.

6

Six green frogs chorused,
Ree-dit, ree-dit,
from the mossy walls
inside a wishing well.

7

Seven frogs sang deep: **Blu-urp, blu-urp,**
from the side of a road where it curved out of sight.

8

Eight bullfrogs boomed,
WOOMP, WOOMP,
from water running dark
beneath a bridge.

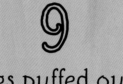

9

Nine green frogs puffed out their throats
to sing, **Gree-deep**, like bumps on a log.

10

Ten frogs trilled, Peep, peep,
from lily pads shining in a pool.

Grunts and croaks, chirps and ribbits.
Low and deep, high and shrill.
All the frogs sang for love.
Until . . .

one car splashed down the wet street,
wheels slooshing along the pavement.
Then . . .

10

Ten frogs stopped peeping
from the lily pads.

9

Nine frogs ka-plopped
off the floating log.

8

Eight frogs
peeked from the dark
beneath the bridge.

7 Seven frogs plunged into the high grass without a rustle to show where they hid.

6 Six frogs hushed inside the mossy wishing well.

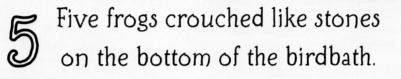

 5 Five frogs crouched like stones
on the bottom of the birdbath.

4 Four frogs pretended
to be part of the bark on the tree.

Three frogs huddled
in the puddle on the path.

Two frogs slipped
down the glassy
windowpane.

1

One frog sprang
from the high garden wall.

The engine rumble faded.
Only the wind made a sound,
whispering across the grass.
The moon wondered down
on the stillness.

Until . . .

One frog leaped
onto the high garden wall
and began to sing . . .

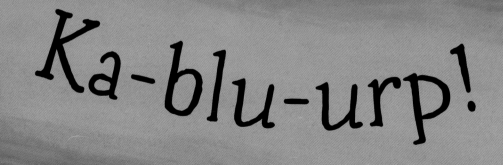

Ka-blu-urp!

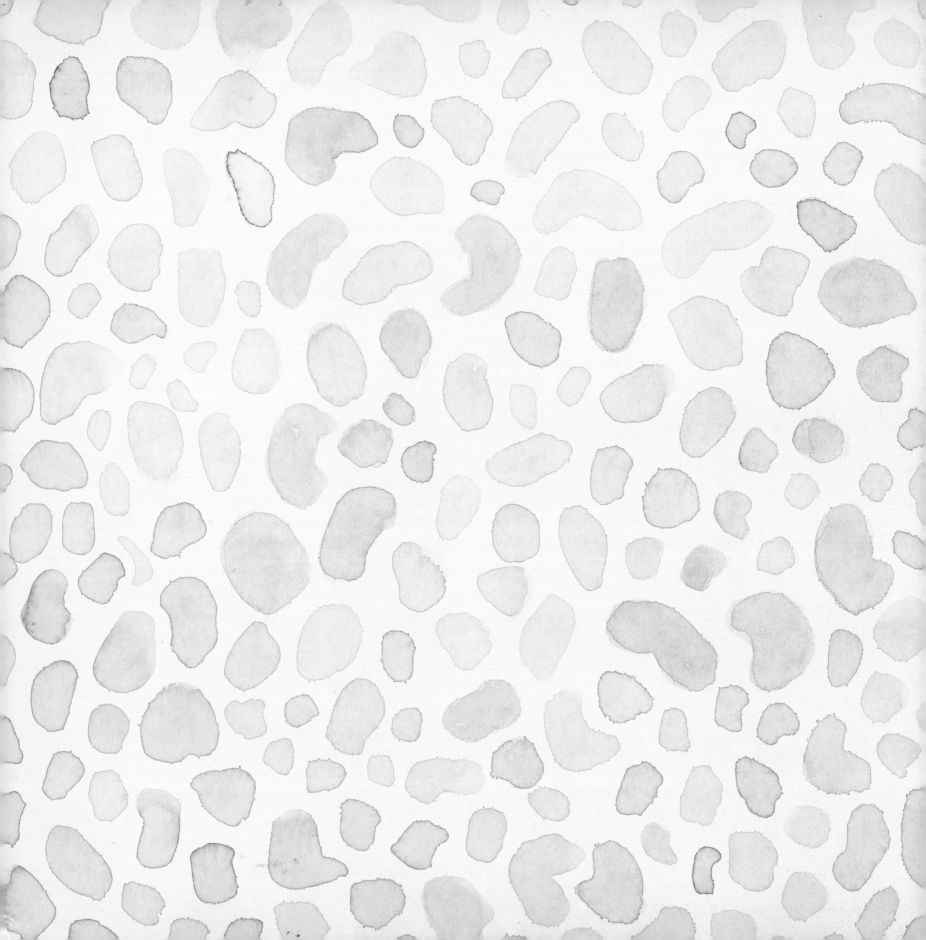